Puffin Books

Editor: Kaye Webb

The WOMBLES Gift Book

All your favourite Womble characters are gathered
together in one volume to be your companions
through the year. Learn how to make MacWomble
shortbread, and read the exciting story of the heroic
part the Scottish Wombles played in the escape of
Bonnie Prince Charlie over the sea to Skye. Learn
some practical Womble magic, and discover how
the Wombles brighten their burrow for spring. Find
out how to make rubbings and lots of other spare-
time pursuits, and while away the hours of darkness
with a Womble story. In fact, Womble the year
away with *The Wombles Gift Book*. Illustrated by
Margaret Gordon and with diagrams and plans
to help you.

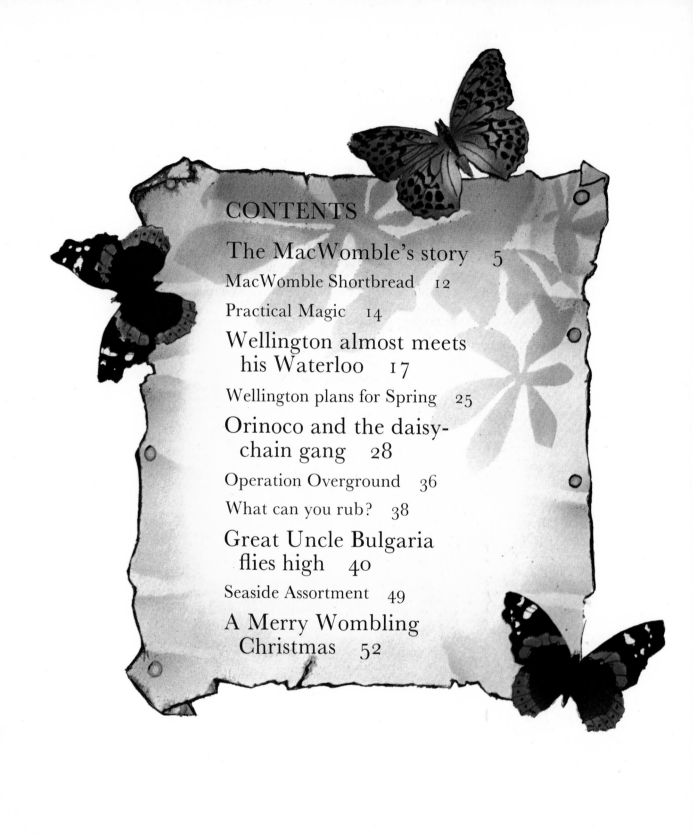

CONTENTS

The MacWomble's story   5

MacWomble Shortbread   12

Practical Magic   14

Wellington almost meets his Waterloo   17

Wellington plans for Spring   25

Orinoco and the daisy-chain gang   28

Operation Overground   36

What can you rub?   38

Great Uncle Bulgaria flies high   40

Seaside Assortment   49

A Merry Wombling Christmas   52

The WOMBLES Gift Book

ELISABETH BERESFORD

Illustrations based on original film puppets
designed by IVOR WOOD © FilmFair Ltd 1972

Drawn by MARGARET GORDON

Other drawings and collage by
Derek Collard

PUFFIN BOOKS

Puffin Books
Penguin Books Ltd, Harmondsworth,
Middlesex, England
Penguin Books Australia Ltd, Ringwood,
Victoria, Australia
Penguin Books Canada Ltd,
41 Steelcase Road West, Markham, Ontario, Canada
Penguin Books (N.Z.) Ltd,
182–190 Wairau Road,
Auckland 10, New Zealand

First published by Puffin Books 1975

Copyright © Elisabeth Beresford, 1975
Illustrations copyright © Margaret Gordon, 1975 and
© Ernest Benn Limited, 1975

Illustrations based on original film puppets designed
by Ivor Wood © FilmFair Ltd 1972

Made and printed in Great Britain by
Jarrold and Sons Ltd, Norwich
Set in Monophoto Baskerville

This book is sold subject to the condition that
it shall not, by way of trade or otherwise, be lent,
re-sold, hired out, or otherwise circulated without
the publisher's prior consent in any form of
binding or cover other than that in which it is
published and without a similar condition
including this condition being imposed on the
subsequent purchaser

The MacWomble's story

'WHAT I WANT TO KNOW,' said Bungo – who is *always* wanting to know something – 'What I want to know is, *why* do the Scottish Wombles wear kilts? After all, we Wombles are covered in fur, so we don't feel the cold. Except for Great Uncle Bulgaria, of course, and that's only because he's so very old and . . .'

'I heard that, young Womble,' said Great Uncle Bulgaria, who had come into the Workshop at this particular moment. 'I may be very old, but my ears are sharp enough. Ho hum!'

5

Bungo shuffled his feet and looked sideways at Great Uncle Bulgaria who was sitting down and pulling his MacWomble tartan shawl more closely round his old shoulders. It was a very cold and windy night and they could just hear the whistling of the wind outside as it howled across the Common. But inside the burrow it was warm and snug and just the sort of evening on which to hear a nice, frightening story. So Great Uncle Bulgaria looked over the top of his spectacles at Cairngorm, the MacWomble the Terrible, who was cleaning his bagpipes and humming under his breath, and he said:

'Yes, Cairngorm, why do you Scottish Wombles wear kilts and all the rest of the paraphernalia, hm?'

'Well now,' said the MacWomble, 'if you really want to know, this is how it all came about. Are you listening carefully?' Great Uncle Bulgaria and Bungo nodded.

'Well,' said the MacWomble . . .

A long, long time ago, way up in Scotland, the Wombles heard that Human Beings were, as quite often happened, having all kinds of fights and troubles between themselves. The Wombles didn't take much notice since they'd got more important things to do, like tidying up, and playing Highland-and-Lowland Games, talking and generally enjoying themselves. That is until one night on one of the islands of the Hebrides, when a very young Womble returned to his burrow looking very upset indeed.

'What's the matter with you?' asked his Womble Chieftain. 'Your tidy-bag's no full and your fur's all up on end. Speak up, wee Womble.'

'There's a lot of trouble up at the Big House. Human Beings whispering and crying and carrying on and they all look so worried,' replied the wee Womble, giving a great sniff.

'Away with you,' said the Chieftain. 'Human Beings are always behaving like that. Now come and sit down and have your porridge and stop fretting. I'll go and have a look myself later on this night.'

The Chieftain was as good as his word and, although he was a big, burly Womble, he was quieter than a fieldmouse as he listened outside the Big House on that stormy night. He had very sharp ears, too, for he could hear what the Human Beings were saying above the shrill whistle of the wind.

'We'll never get you away, Sir,' a lady was saying. 'We've not got a boat that's seaworthy. I've a pass to the Mainland for myself, a manservant, an Irish spinning maid called Betty and a boat's crew of six. All that's fine. But we haven't the boat . . .'

7

'Then I'm done for,' said the gentleman. He was tall and thin, but he looked sort of noble, and the Womble Chieftain could see that he had an air of authority. 'My enemies'll capture me here, like a rat is caught in a trap. And once they've got me, I'll be imprisoned, brought to trial and then my life's no worth a candle . . .'

'Tck, tck, tck,' said the Womble to himself. 'What a silly lot these Human Beings are to be sure. Not looking after their boats indeed. Well, well, we can't have anything like this going on here. Human Beings caught like rats and killed. Nonsense! As usual, we Wombles will have to come to the rescue. I'd best be on my way to the Workshop to see what can be done to make a seaworthy boat. Tck, tck, tck . . .'

Away went the Womble Chieftain, back to his burrow, where he called together all his working Wombles and made a little speech.

'I don't know, nor do I want to, what these Human Beings are about, but we'll have no trouble on this island as long as I'm Chieftain here. I know where the Human Beings have

left an old boat. You must all of you put your paws to work and collect bits of driftwood and old nails and such-like stuff. Then, with that rubbish, we'll make the boat seaworthy. Do you understand?'

All the Hebridean Wombles nodded and then, with no more words spoken, they set to work. One group went off to look for the boat and another group sorted through all the bits and pieces in the Workshop. They gathered together tar, calico, wood, nails and ends of rope which they wove together. They all worked and worked till their backs ached and their paws were scratchy and their eyes were blurred. But by dawn, as the wind began to turn, there was a very stout, seaworthy boat on the shore.

The Womble Chieftain, whose grey fur was all tufty and bedraggled from lack of sleep and hard work, shivered. He had never felt the cold before and for a moment he wondered if he was getting very old. Then he looked at all his younger working Wombles who had been labouring for so long, and he saw that their fur was ragged too.

'Tck, tck, tck,' said the Womble Chieftain and he squared his shoulders and marched straight up to the Big House, and put a letter under the door and knocked very loudly. Then he took cover. A lady came out a few moments later and put a hand up to her eyes. She seemed to have been crying, but when she saw the mended seaworthy boat her whole face lit up. She turned and ran back into the Big House calling at the top of her voice:

'Sir, Sir, we have friends indeed on this island *and* we have a boat! Rouse everybody, quick, quick. The wind has turned . . . Sir, you can escape after all . . . !'

The working Wombles, all scratchy and itchy from over-work and lack of sleep, watched silently as a small party of Human Beings came out of the Big House and crunched down to the shore. All of them got into the boat and then, just before it was pushed out to sea, the very last person, who looked like a rather tall, awkward sort of pretending-to-be-a-female Human Being, paused.

This Human Being got off the boat and came crunching back across the pebbles and then stopped just short of the bushes where the Wombles were watching and hiding.

'I don't know who you are, friends,' said the person, 'but I thank you. I shall never forget you, no matter what happens. From this day forwards you may have the right to wear my tartan. Call it what you will. My name – my friends – underneath this disguise, is Charles Edward Stuart.'

The Human Being bowed low as he spoke and the Womble Chieftain stepped out from his hiding place and bowed too. And for a moment the two of them looked at each other, neither of them at their best in appearance, and then they bowed and smiled again.

Ten minutes later the seaworthy boat was only a black blob on the choppy sea . . .

'I do believe,' said Great Uncle Bulgaria, 'that the wind has blown itself out. What a very interesting story, Cairngorm. I'd no idea that Himself, Prince Charles Edward Stuart, granted us the right to the MacWomble tartan. Goodness me, those were stirring times. Ho hum. And so we had a paw, so to speak, in the escape of Prince Charles from the Hebrides. Dear me . . .'

'What *I* want to know,' said Bungo, 'is the name of the wee Womble who started the whole story.'

'Benbecula, what else?' said the MacWomble. 'For that was the place from which Bonnie Prince Charlie escaped. Now come and give me a paw with cleaning these bagpipes, young Bungo. Tck, tck, tck, you're a lazy lot, you young Wombles, so you are!'

MacWomble Shortbread

'We do have another connection with the Stuart family,' said the MacWomble, later on that evening, when they were all sitting comfortably by the fire.

'One afternoon, many many years ago when Mary Queen of Scots was quite a young girl (she was the great-great-great-grandmother of Bonnie Prince Charlie), she was feeling terribly bored. It was raining, so she couldn't go outside and everything in Stirling Castle seemed very dull. So she went by herself into the Great Kitchens to see if there was anything she could do. But there was nobody there – except a small Womble who had bravely slipped in to see if there was anything no one wanted that a careful Womble could use for supper. Mary Stuart didn't see her at first, of course, but the wee Womble heard her sighing, and so she plucked up courage to speak to her. Being a queen, even if only a very young one, she was used to coming to terms quickly with things she didn't quite understand, and the two got on very well together.

'The wee Womble, who later became famous in Womble history when she wrote THE WOMBLE BOOK OF HOUSEHOLD MANAGEMENT with lots of recipes in it that were entirely her own invention, suggested doing a little cooking to pass the time. Together, they worked out a completely new recipe. The beauty of it was that it was quite simple.' The MacWomble paused. 'I should ask Madame Cholet. I'm sure she knows how to make Mary Stuart's Petticoat Tails, or as we call it, the MacWomble Shortbread.'

He was quite right: and Madame Cholet was only too pleased to have helpers in the kitchen! This is how she explained the recipe:

Recipe for MacWomble Shortbread

YOU WILL NEED
8 oz sifted flour
4 oz butter
2 heaped tablespoonfuls caster sugar
3 tablespoonfuls milk
oven setting: 350 °F electric
No. 4 gas

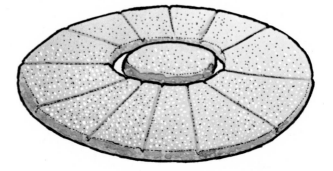

WHAT YOU DO

1. Melt the butter in the milk.

2. Then make a well in the centre of the flour, and pour in the butter and milk, adding the sugar.

3. Stir all the ingredients together and knead a little to make sure everything is well mixed.

4. Put the biscuit mixture on to a lightly floured board and roll out to 6 mm thickness.

5. Now put a dinner plate upside down on top, and cut round the edge, so that you have a circle. Put a wine glass in the middle and cut round that; now you have a round hole in the middle. Save the circle you have cut out.

6. Divide what is remaining into segments. Do not cut right through the mixture, just make deep cuts. Bake with the roundel you have cut out on a lightly greased baking tin for about twenty minutes, or until golden brown. Cool on a wire rack, dust with caster sugar and serve with the round cake in the middle and the 'petticoat tails' around it.

Practical Magic

One evening a few days later, it was particularly cold, wet and blustery. The Wombles were all sitting drinking a hot creamy hazelnut nightcap and eating what remained of the petticoat tails. The MacWomble smiled as he said slowly to Great Uncle Bulgaria:

'Many's the long cold night I've spent sitting in the firelight, glad of our nice warm Scottish burrow. When the day's work is done, we often sit and tell stories——'

'Yes, we know *that*,' whispered Bungo a bit rudely.

'*And,*' went on the MacWomble, ignoring the interruption, 'we sometimes do a bit of practical magic.'

There was an awed hush.

'Well,' said Great Uncle Bulgaria, smiling too, 'perhaps we English Wombles know a bit as well. I know my old friend Tobermory has some thoughts on this himself . . .'

Nobody knows *exactly* how some of the MacWomble's magic works, but here are a few of the things they did that you might like to try.

Self Supporting Water

YOU WILL NEED

1. A drinking glass (This works best if the glass is not too thick.)
2. A piece of thin card, a bit bigger than the rim of the glass

1. Fill the glass to overflowing with water.

2. Slide the card over the rim of the glass, making sure that the glass is as airtight as possible.

3. Now quickly turn the glass upside down and take your hand away from the card. The water will not come out – but practice makes perfect and this is a trick that is best tried first over a basin or bath!

Control Your Own Diver

YOU WILL NEED

1. The empty refill tube of an old ball-point pen, cut to a length of 4 cm

2. Candle wax

3. A piece of 10 amp. fuse wire about 16 cm long

4. A glass of water

5. A bottle with a cork (Make sure the cork is airtight.)

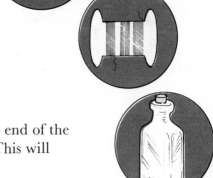

WHAT YOU DO

1. Melt a little candle wax and dip one end of the ball-point refill tube in it to seal it. This will be the top end of your diver.

2. Now coil the fuse wire tightly round the refill tube near the opposite end to the one you have sealed, and drop it into the glass of water. If there is enough fuse wire, it should sink slowly to the bottom, staying upright. Take off a little of the fuse wire at a time until the tube will just rise slowly from the bottom of the glass.

3. Fill your bottle to the top with water. Very carefully, take your diver out of the glass of water and drop him in the bottle.

15

4. Push in the cork. Then raise it very gently (but do not take it out), and watch what happens. You can control your diver by gently raising and lowering the cork. If he gets stuck at the bottom, take him out, shake out the surplus water and drop him in again.

How not to Burst a Balloon

YOU WILL NEED

1. A balloon and a small piece of sticky tape.

WHAT YOU DO

1. Blow up the balloon and stick the tape firmly anywhere on the surface.

2. Now take a pin and stick it into the balloon, through the tape. Nothing happens! The pin stays in the balloon and your friends, who probably thought you were in for a nasty shock, will be mystified.

Invisible Ink

YOU WILL NEED

1. Paper

2. Milk or lemon juice

WHAT YOU DO

1. This is very simple, but very effective. If you have a message that you want only Certain People to read, write it in lemon juice or milk on a sheet of white paper. Let your 'ink' dry, put the note in an envelope and send it. If the note falls into the wrong hands, it doesn't matter because they will see only a sheet of blank paper and be extremely puzzled. When your friend receives it, however, all he or she has to do is warm the paper. Magically the message will show up in brown letters.

Wellington almost meets his Waterloo

'I'M GLAD THE WINTER IS OVER, because I think I like it best on Wimbledon Common when it's springtime,' said Wellington.

'I don't,' said Orinoco. 'It's a funny thing about spring, it always makes *me* feel sleepier than ever. The squirrels won't keep still for a minute, the birds won't stop singing – well they call it singing, but I call it a lot of shouting – and even the moles and hedgehogs start rushing about. It's all VERY tiring and . . .'

'And wet,' said Tomsk, who had just come into the burrow. He shook himself violently and sent a shower of water over Orinoco who sighed deeply and then went off to the kitchen to see if it was 'elevenses' time. Oddly enough it was quite damp in the kitchen too.

'Is it still raining?' asked Wellington. Tomsk shook himself again and then said in his slow way:

'It's not raining from the sky. The sky up above, you know. THAT sky. It's just wet all round. The trees and the bushes and the grass are full of wetness, and Queen's Mere is EVER so wet and so are the banks leading down to it. It's all so wet that I can't play golf or go for a nice run – too much mud – so it's all very dull on the Common with nothing to do but

pick up rubbish. It's jolly wet in here too . . . I say, Wellington, where are you going?'

Tomsk spoke to the empty air, for Wellington had hurried out of the burrow with his tidy-bag under one arm, muttering to himself:

'If he says wet once more I'll go barmy. I don't care whatever the other Wombles say, I *like* the spring. It smells lovely for one thing . . .'

Wellington took a deep breath, which misted up his spectacles so that he had to take them off and wipe them on his scarf. It was true that the Common was covered in a kind of damp mist, but apart from that there was a lovely fresh smell in the air. There was a lot to look at too, for there were buds and blossom everywhere, the grass was a bright, new green and the early flowers were adding little bits of colour up and down the slopes of the Common.

'Yes I *do* like Wimbledon Common when it's springtime,' Wellington said to himself, 'I like it because . . . goodness what's THAT?'

He stopped and listened. 'That' was a very unusual sound. The sound of a great deal of water moving at high speed. It was as if a big river had suddenly chosen to roll across the Common. As Wellington, like all the Wombles, was very inquisitive he went running across the grass, sniffing and looking and listening as hard as he could go, until he got to the high banks above Queen's Mere and there a very strange sight met his eyes. Water was pouring, rushing and bumping and splashing down at least six small ravines, until they frothed into the Mere. 'Mm that looks lovely,' said Wellington. 'How jolly exciting – OOh!' This last remark was caused by the fact that he could see that by no means all the water was going into the Mere. A steadily growing stream was creeping sideways – right in the direction of the burrow! Something must have got gummed up somewhere and unless he did

something quickly, a great deal of water was going to be channelled straight into the Wombles' home.

'Help,' said Wellington and took to his back paws as fast as he could go. He slid and scampered across the Common until with a great squelching sound he reached the front door just as Tomsk, still looking rather damp, came out.

'I wondered where you'd got to,' Tomsk said. 'You look ever so wet and . . .'

'Wet, 'course I'm wet,' replied Wellington, catching his breath in great gasps, because he wasn't as athletic as Tomsk and not used to running so fast. 'Everything on the Common is dripping wet and underwater, too, in some bits. Where's Great Uncle Bulgaria and Tobermory and Bungo and Orinoco and Madame Cholet and everybody? Quick, it's urgent and important.'

'Out,' said Tomsk, 'everybody's out, but me. There's been so much rain that a lot of rubbish has been washed down the roads and on to the Common. It's been all paws to the pump to clear up. I'm the only Womble left in the burrow, which is not very nice because there's water all over the floor. I don't like it. We've never had water all over the floor before, you know.'

Tomsk stopped speaking, almost as out of breath as Wellington, because Tomsk has never been a very talkative Womble. It's only when he gets really worried that he can talk much.

'Oh dear, oh dear, OH DEAR!' said Wellington. Tomsk didn't speak. He had used up all his words for the time being, so he just shook himself again and, even after all this time,

his fur was so damp that he sent little plip-plops of wetness flying into the air.

Wellington looked at Tomsk's shiny fur and then at the tiny rivulets of water which were oozing into the corridor and his own fur went into little spiky tufts. Not out of dampness, but because he was suddenly very scared. Apart from Tomsk he was quite alone and he was also quite, quite sure that the burrow was in danger of being flooded. So Wellington put his head between his hands and shut his eyes and thought as hard as he possibly could while Tomsk watched him. Tomsk was worried, too, but he didn't perfectly understand what was happening; he only knew that Wellington was clever enough to deal with the danger.

'Yes, that's it,' Wellington said suddenly, 'I remember the way the Common slopes. It's just got to be changed, that's all. Come on, Tomsk.'

'Are we going to change the way the Common goes up and down?' asked Tomsk rather fearfully. It seemed a very large sort of job.

'No, we're going to dig canals,' said Wellington. 'Get two big spades and hurry up, do, there's a good Womble.'

Once Wellington had got everything worked out in his mind, he knew exactly what had to be done, and luckily for him he had Tomsk with him. So Wellington directed and Tomsk dug furiously, and within quite a short time a little channel had been dug sideways from the main stream. Water started rushing down in a stronger and stronger flood until Tomsk soon found that all the earth was sliding from under his paws. 'Oops,' he panted, as he nearly sat down in the middle of the stream, 'I can't do this much more.'

'Well, we must go sideways *again*,' directed Wellington briskly. Secretly, he was rather enjoying being in charge,

especially as Tomsk seemed to think he would know exactly what to do. 'You see, we have got to divert the water into the Mere,' he said importantly.

'Ah,' said Tomsk. He was so busy digging he hadn't any breath to say anything else, and anyway, he had a feeling that he would only get muddled even if Wellington explained it ever so carefully. Slowly, slowly, the stream stopped creeping in the direction of the burrow. Instead, it was splashing down the new channels made by the two young Wombles and straight towards Queen's Mere. It was messy, muddy and wet work, but the two young Wombles worked furiously and really they quite enjoyed it, because it is fun building lovely messy dams and diverting water – especially when you know you are saving your home by doing so.

When the last dam had been built and the water was frothing and bubbling down into the Mere, Wellington leant on his spade and gave an enormous, great happy sigh. The burrow was saved. It wouldn't, couldn't be flooded now; all the rain and puddles were going to where they belonged – into the Mere.

'I think I'll go for a walk,' said Wellington.

'O.K.,' replied Tomsk. 'I'm going to try water-sliding. That old plank will just do fine.'

Which is how, when all the other Wombles, very wet and muddy, returned to their nice dry burrow, there was no sign of Tomsk or Wellington.

'It's not fair,' grumbled Orinoco. 'Here's all of us been working and working AND WORKING . . . and over there is Tomsk doing water-sliding . . .'

'Water *what*?' said Great Uncle Bulgaria. 'Dear me, Tomsk has invented a new water sport. And very good at it he is, too!'

'While Wellington's just looking at flowers,' said Orinoco, who had just spotted his other friend.

'Um, um, um,' said Great Uncle Bulgaria, whose sharp old eyes had begun to notice all kinds of tracks, rivulets and signs of hard work. 'Well I daresay that both Tomsk and Wellington have been working most diligently while we have been away. Dear, dear me, spring weather has its good and bad sides. Everything always seems to happen at once at this time of year. It's all *very* exhausting . . .'

'Yes, isn't it?' said Orinoco. 'It makes *me* feel ever so tired too . . .'

The other Wombles all agreed with him, that is except Wellington who, in spite of his particularly tiring day, during which he (and Tomsk) had saved the burrow from being flooded, said very, very firmly, 'I like it best on Wimbledon Common when it's springtime, BECAUSE there's so much happening!'

24

Wellington plans for Spring

Spring Gardens

'I *like* spring,' said Wellington happily to himself as he opened up the front door of the burrow early one morning in April. 'There is so much to see and everything is creeping and growing and bursting out in a new, clean sort of way.' He sang in a rather tuneless monotone, but it showed how he was feeling. All the Wombles were working on a new scheme of Great Uncle Bulgaria's – a Great Womble Spring Cleaning. And Wellington had a very particular plan of his own to brighten up the burrow.

Not everyone has a garden to grow things in, but nearly everyone has a spare window sill or step they can use. A pot of flowers really will brighten up your own special place, as well as being great fun to watch growing.

YOU WILL NEED

Either

1. A plastic window box, and a pair of
   metal brackets to fix it to your window
   sill
   Or a wooden box (You can try asking your local
   greengrocer if he has any old fruit, vegetable or
   seed boxes. Otherwise, go to a garden shop.)
   Some thin sheets of wood
   Or a wire basket from the garden shop
   (Wellington used an old chip basket, but you may
   not be lucky enough to find one of these.)
   Or a small barrel cut in half

Or

2. Some pots, and containers of any sort: yoghurt pots, flower pots, plastic squash containers cut in half. (You will probably need someone to help you do this.) An old bucket, or even an old sink, would also make a good container but make sure that it does not have any jagged edges

3. A mixture of peat, garden soil or leaf mould

4. Stones or moss

5. Plants. The best ones to start with are primulas, wallflowers and alyssum. Coming slightly later in the year are marigolds, daisies, pansies, virginia stock, geraniums and candytuft. You can buy them at a garden shop

WHAT YOU DO

1. To make your plant box, you must first make sure that the sides and base of your box are strong enough to hold the weight of soil, so nail the thin sheets of wood crosswise on the bottom and along the cracks in the sides (see illustration). Leave some slits in the bottom for the water to drain through. This will stop your box from getting waterlogged.

2. If you are using containers, clean them thoroughly. This is very important, as whatever was in them before may not agree with your plants and so spoil your garden.

3. Make holes in the bottom of your containers. If they are made of plastic, you can do this with a corkscrew or a screwdriver. (Be careful: they are sharp!) You will need someone to help you drill holes in the bottom of the barrel.

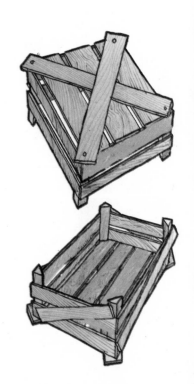

4. Now you can paint your box or barrel with different colours and patterns, but do remember to use waterproof paint. You could even put some putty on the box and stick shells or coloured stones in the putty for decoration. Then varnish it to make it look glossy. The paint and varnish, as well as looking pretty, will help to make your box weatherproof. The smaller containers have lots of possibilities too. Try sticking on coloured paper shapes. Metal foil looks especially good.

5. At this point, if you are using a window box, you will need to get someone to help you fix it to the sill with the bracket. You MUST make sure that it is very securely fastened.

6. Now put moss in the bottom of your basket, or small stones in your barrel, box or containers. This is to help the water drain away out of the bottom. The containers should be standing in an old tray to catch the extra water.

Sieve the soil or leaf mould and peat and put it on top of the stones until the containers are two-thirds full. Don't pack it down too hard. Now carefully put in the plants, patting the rest of the soil firmly round the roots. You will have to water your plants straight away, so you will be able to check your drainage system!

Now water the plants every time the soil is dry to the touch, and before long you will see new leaves and buds opening out.

You must make sure that your plants have plenty of light as well as water. If you cut off the dead flower heads, your plants will bloom longer, and if you are careful, they should last all the summer.

Orinoco and
the daisy-chain gang

'SUMMERTIME,' SANG ORINOCO, somewhat off-key, 'good old summertime. Nothing to do when my work is done, but lie and snooze in the nice warm suuuuuuuuuun.'

Orinoco gave a happy sigh of contentment. He had actually got up enough energy to make himself a tree house. It wasn't very well built, in fact Tobermory would have had a fit if he had seen it, but then neither he nor any of the other Wombles – except one – knew that the house existed. The idea of making it had come to Orinoco quite suddenly when he had been woken up for at least the twentieth time while having a lovely forty winks under a bramble bush.

'The trouble is,' Orinoco had muttered crossly under his breath, 'that everybody knows where they can get AT me when there's more work to be done, bother it. What I need is a very special, secret place where none of 'em can find me. What I need . . . what I need is my own private tree house!'

The other Wombles would have been astonished, if they could have seen how hard Orinoco had worked to make his private tree house. He had even got up ten minutes early in the morning to go looking for pieces of wood and armfuls of dried bracken and lengths of string. By the end of six days he had cobbled together his little, rather wobbly, but very cosy shelter. It was balanced between two strong branches very near the top of a tree and it had a floor, three walls, half a ceiling and a lot of lovely, dry, cosy bracken as a bed. Orinoco thought it was perfect.

'Summertime . . .' he sang again, blinking sleepily at the sunny shafts which were shining through the roof, 'peace and quiet . . . a nice forty winks . . . what more can a Womble ask for? And Orinoco went fast asleep.

Orinoco slept so well that he had not just forty winks, but a good eighty, which meant that he was late back to the burrow. What was even worse, he was so late that there was hardly any supper left for him.

'Poor Orinoco,' said Madame Cholet. 'There is some acorn and bramble stew, but the daisy ice-cream is all finished.'

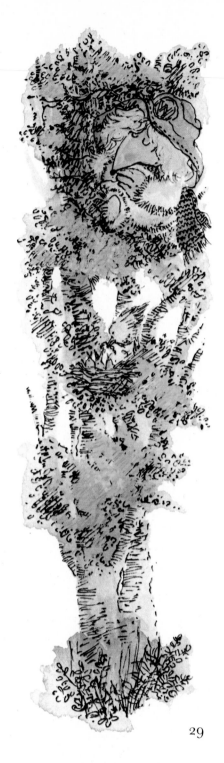

'Finished!' cried Orinoco. 'But daisy ice-cream is my favourite pudding. Well, one of my favourite puddings.'

'It had hot buttercup sauce with it too,' said Madame Cholet. 'All bubbling and golden. It was quite delicious . . .'

'And that's all eaten up *too*!' exclaimed Orinoco. 'That's definitely not *fair*! Daisy ice-cream with hot, bubbly buttercup sauce, now that IS my favourite pudding. Why wasn't there enough to go round, Madame Cholet?'

'We are very short of both the daisies and the buttercups,' said Madame Cholet as she dished up the acorn and bramble stew. 'All the young Wombles are working so hard at clearing up rubbish while it is the summer. The Human Beings leave a great deal of litter behind them at this time, as you know Orinoco, so that when you all finish work you are too tired to go picking flowers, yes?'

'Yes, well, sort of,' said Orinoco, shuffling his paws a bit, because he felt just a shade guilty. 'Is there any more stew?'

'Alas no,' replied Madame Cholet, 'but if you are still hungry you can have some grass buns with acorn spread.'

'I suppose that'll have to do,' said Orinoco.

'*Pardon!*' exclaimed Madame Cholet in a stern French accent. '*Pardon!*'

'I mean, yes, thank you very much,' Orinoco said hurriedly. 'I like your grass buns and acorn spread a lot. Only it's not quite the same as daisy ice-cream and hot buttercup sauce . . .'

Madame Cholet's eyes twinkled, but she didn't say anything, she just hummed softly to herself as she put the nearly empty glass jars which were labelled 'DAISIES – DRIED' and 'BUTTERCUP-MIX', straight on the shelves . . .

30

The next day Orinoco was quite determined not to have more than forty winks. But it was so deliciously quiet and warm and sunny up in his little tree house that he just dozed straight off yet again, and if the truth were told he snored and scratched and slumbered for at least seventy-nine winks. It was the rumbling of his own round stomach which woke him up and, as he blinked and stretched, he noticed first the white and gold patches of the daisies and buttercups in the grass beneath him, and then the long shadows which meant that it was past supper-time. With a speed surprising in one of his build Orinoco made for the burrow.

What a delicious smell greeted him.

'Bramble and bracken pie,' murmured Orinoco, taking a deep, deep breath. 'And – yes – I do believe it's buttercup roly-poly with daisy cream . . . oooooooo. . .!'

'Orinoco,' exclaimed Madame Cholet, 'at last. You poor little Womble working so hard and such long, long hours. How unfair life is to be sure. *Alors!*'

'What – what do you mean?' inquired Orinoco, his fur rising up in little tufts of anxiety.

'There is only a *petit* helping of pie remaining and – oh how can I bear to tell you – no roly-poly and cream at all. But there are plenty of buns and spread with which you can fill up the corners of your stomach.'

Orinoco didn't say anything. He felt both dreadfully disappointed and very guilty at the same time and it took all the words out of him. Although he was longing and aching for an enormous helping of pie and two enormous helpings of roly-poly, he knew that he didn't really deserve them, because the others *had* been working while he'd been fast asleep.

Orinoco heaved a sigh which made him quiver from head to paw. Madame Cholet shook her head in sympathy and then put the empty daisy and buttercup jars into the sink.

32

The next day was a holiday, but a very, very thoughtful Orinoco did two rather unusual things. He borrowed an alarm clock from Tobermory's Workshop and he took two tidy-bags off their pegs.

'Dear me,' said Great Uncle Bulgaria, whose sharp old eyes had noticed these unusual actions. 'Very strange. Well, well I mustn't detain him at this moment as he is looking most determined about something or other. Most. I want to have a word with all the working Wombles tonight about a little summer scheme of mine, in which they will have an exciting break from tidying up and learn to live not underground, but *over*ground. But I do wonder, what is Orinoco up to, eh Madame Cholet?'

Madame Cholet shrugged in a very French way, her shoulders coming up to her ears. All she said was:

'*Up* to? Who can say, Bulgaria . . .'

Orinoco climbed up to his private tree house, set the alarm clock and fell fast asleep. A mere twenty winks later the alarm was buzzing like an angry bee and Orinoco, yawning, scratching and sighing, turned it off, put the clock into one of the tidy-bags and slid down the tree. Then he began to pick daisies. He knew exactly where to go because he had got such a good view of them from his little nest. When the tidy-bag was full to the brim he sighed again and made for the place where the best, most golden buttercups were growing. He picked and picked AND PICKED until the second tidy-bag was bursting with flowers and then he ambled back to the burrow. He didn't notice Great Uncle Bulgaria, because that elderly Womble was sitting quietly in his rocking-chair in the shade of a bramble bush. But Great Uncle Bulgaria saw Orinoco, in fact he had been watching him all the afternoon.

'Ho hum, dear me, well, well,' said Great Uncle Bulgaria. 'Now I understand what's been going on! And how useful this information will be when I give my little talk this evening about going camping. Ho ho ho, hum hum.'

And Great Uncle Bulgaria chuckled to himself so much that his chair rocked backwards and forwards quite violently and nearly tipped him into the bramble bush.

'Orinoco!' exclaimed Madame Cholet when she saw the two bulging tidy-bags. '*Magnifique!* So many daisies, so much buttercup. *Tiens* and *alors*, also. You are a good, hard-working, kind Womble. I shall tell all the others what you have done.'

'I'd rather you didn't,' mumbled Orinoco. He shuffled his paws and then looked up at Madame Cholet whose little round eyes were twinkling like anything.

34

'Ah,' said Madame Cholet, 'I think perhaps I understand. Sometimes when it is summer one wishes to doze and dream in peace and quiet, but alas, it is not always possible. Work has to be done if the Common is to be kept clean and neat and small round stomachs have to be filled. Yes?'

Orinoco thought this over and then it did occur to him that perhaps Madame Cholet, when she had been out picking flowers, might just have glanced up and noticed a – well – a little private tree house?

'I say,' said Orinoco, shuffling more than ever, 'you won't tell, you won't let on that . . .'

'*Pardon?*' said Madame Cholet in a very French voice. 'You were saying? Oh never mind *pour le moment* as there is so much to be done. And the first of these is to make you a little something special as a reward for all your hard work. Perhaps some daisy ice-cream with . . .'

Orinoco sighed again, only this time it was a happy sigh.

'. . . hot, golden buttercup sauce?' he said.

'*Exactement!*' agreed Madame Cholet and she began cooking immediately.

Operation Overground

That evening, just as he promised, Great Uncle Bulgaria gathered together a band of scuffling, bright-eyed young Wombles, all curious as to what 'Operation Overground' was going to be.

'As you will have guessed,' said Great Uncle Bulgaria when the scuffling had subsided, 'Operation Overground is to do with living out-doors. And you will be glad to know that one of our Wombles has already pioneered the way . . .' (Orinoco started guiltily.)

'I think you will all enjoy camping, as well as find out a great deal more about the Common,' Great Uncle Bulgaria went on. And here is some-thing the Wombles did the very next day.

Your Own Tent

Some people may be lucky enough to own a small tent, but even if you haven't got one, it is still great fun to improvise.

YOU WILL NEED

1. An old sheet or blanket; or if you are lucky enough to find it, a square of canvas
2. A tarpaulin, or length of plastic waterproof sheeting for the groundsheet
3. Some bricks or stones: or several tent pegs, or pointed pieces of wood, and a hammer
4. A clothes line or length of rope

WHAT YOU DO

1. Put the sheet, blanket or square of canvas over the clothes line (or if you have decided to camp in a wood, and not in your back garden, you can easily stretch your rope between two trees). Make sure that at least 15 cm of the material is lying on the ground. It is best to lay the waterproof sheeting inside your tent at this point, as it is difficult to do later on. Keep the material as tightly stretched as possible (or your tent will sag). Now weight the material down with a couple of bricks or stones, or peg it into the ground with the tent pegs or pointed sticks.

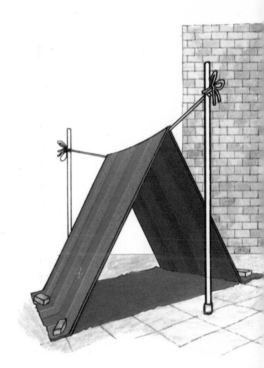

Or

2. Tie your rope to the branch of a tree, about a metre off the ground. Now make the other end of your rope secure with one of the tent pegs, about 1·3 metres away from the tree. Make sure that the rope is tight. Then put your blanket, sheet or square of canvas over the rope, as before, and fix the two ends of material that make the entrance with two more tent pegs. Check that the topmost part of the tent is fixed firmly to the rope, so that your tent will not slide down. It is best to choose a tree where you can put the entrance facing away from the wind.

37

Trackers and Indians

Once the Wombles had made themselves a camp, they played lots of different games. *Trackers* is a favourite because it is great fun and very useful for learning how to keep hidden from Human Beings!

WHAT YOU DO

Two people stay at the base camp (they are the trackers) while the rest (the Indians) hide near by. The Indians have to reach home (this can be a tree, wall, etc. near to the base camp) without being seen. The two trackers have to spot and catch the hiding Indians. When they see one of them, they shout out the name of the person and where they saw him. If they are right, then the Indian has to come out into the open and make a dash for the 'home', trying not to get caught by the trackers. If he *is* caught, then he becomes one of the trackers and has to help catch the others.

What can you rub?

Very early on, young Wombles learn to tell the different trees apart, and to help them, Tobermory thought up a very simple method. He took rubbings of the bark and the leaves and pasted them up in the Playroom. You can take rubbings too, and not only from trees – interesting stones and shells work just as well.

If you live in a town, look for old coal-hole covers (they are round metal plates in the pavement) or any surface with a raised pattern on it.

38

You can make simple and very effective pictures this way and you will probably be surprised how many different textures and patterns you can find.

YOU WILL NEED

1. Leaves, stones, shells, bark, coal-hole covers, carved stone, coins, etc. (Obviously, you will have to rub some things where they are!)

2. A *soft* lead pencil (this means it is marked 'B') or wax crayon. Best of all is a brass-rubbing crayon which you can buy from an art shop. You can get them in all sorts of colours too

3. A sheet of white or coloured paper

WHAT YOU DO

1. Turn over your leaf so you can see the veins sticking up. Now put the sheet of paper over the leaf and gently press it flat. Carefully, without tearing the leaf, rub on the paper with the crayon, using smooth even strokes as far as possible. The edge of the leaf and the vein patterns will show up as a solid colour on your paper.

2. You can treat bark in almost exactly the same way, also the man-made things like coal-hole covers. The important thing is not to let the paper move while you are making the rubbing. For large objects it is a good idea to have someone else to hold the paper while you rub, and then, when you get tired, you can swop over.

Great Uncle Bulgaria flies high

TOBERMORY WAS REALLY QUITE WORRIED about Great Uncle Bulgaria, because his old friend was starting to look both very old and very tired after the long, hot and exhausting summer. Tobermory thought things over and one evening he went to have a word with Miss Adelaide, who is in charge of the Womblegarten. Miss Adelaide was sitting and sewing in the kitchen with Madame Cholet, who was drying and preserving stores for the winter. They listened to everything that Tobermory had to say and at the finish Madame Cholet remarked:

'You are perfectly correct, as always, M'sieur Tobermory. Me, I am also worried about my little cook, young Alderney. She has worked so hard all through the summer and now she too is very tired. Tck, tck, tck.'

'It's been a most tiring summer for *all* of us,' agreed Miss Adelaide. 'Even we Wombles cannot work *all* the time. Tomsk has also been overdoing things, he has got a bad case of falling fur, I've noticed. Tck, tck, tck.'

'So what's to be done?' asked Tobermory, adding, 'ta very much,' as Madame Cholet handed him a cup of steaming

hot blackberry juice. 'And *you* don't look yourself either Madame Cholet, if you don't mind me mentioning it.'

'I am a *little* weary,' agreed Madame Cholet. 'One never seems to stop working at this time of year.'

Miss Adelaide finished her sewing, put it to one side and thought hard for a moment, while the other two Wombles looked at her.

'Right!' exclaimed Miss Adelaide so suddenly that the other two Wombles jumped. 'That's it. Of course. How stupid; but then one never does see the answer when it is staring one in the face. Yes, that's it.'

'Is it?' said Tobermory cautiously.

'A holiday. A complete break, that's what's needed,' said Miss Adelaide crisply. 'Great Uncle Bulgaria, Madame Cholet, Alderney and Tomsk must have a holiday.'

'It would be marvellous,' said Madame Cholet, quite forgetting how tired she felt. 'But *where* would one go?'

'Think of your names,' said Miss Adelaide, picking up the next piece of sewing. 'You must go to one of your name-places.'

'Cholet?' said Madame Cholet. 'But would that little town in France be quiet at this time of year? And as for Tomsk, in Russia, that would hardly be sunny and warm now, and Bulgaria is such a large country, which leaves only . . . *Tiens!*'

'Precisely,' said Miss Adelaide. 'All four of you should go

for a holiday on the Channel Island of Alderney! We must start making arrangements immediately!'

Once Miss Adelaide had made up her mind that something should be done, there was no stopping her. She brushed aside all Great Uncle Bulgaria's objections as if they had been thistledown; she told Madame Cholet that she, Miss Adelaide, was perfectly capable of running the kitchen for two weeks with the help of the Womblegarten – as it was high time they got some cooking experience – and as for Alderney, she was so much in awe of Miss Adelaide that she agreed to everything.

Tomsk didn't really understand what all the fuss was about so he kept quiet, until he heard that on the island of Alderney there were often high surfing waves.

'Cor,' said Tomsk, 'you mean I could learn to surf? Cor!'

All the Wimbledon Wombles turned out to see off the departing party who, having been kitted out by Tobermory, had everything they could possibly want.

'Flying!' said Great Uncle Bulgaria. 'It doesn't seem possible that I shall be taking to the air again. Why, I remember the last time . . .'

'Yes, yes, yes,' said Tobermory. 'Come along, Bulgaria old friend, or we won't get to Southampton Airport in time to even *catch* the plane.'

The airport was very quiet with only a few Human Beings travelling, and they were so full of their own affairs that they never spared a second glance for the Wombles.

'It's a very small aeroplane, isn't it?' said Alderney, nervously, as she saw the Islander plane coming in to land.

'All the better to fly in,' said Great Uncle Bulgaria. 'Hang

43

on to my paw, young Womble . . .'

As it happened, all the Wombles held on tightly to each other during the flight, but it was a very smooth journey and when Alderney saw the island after which she had been named appear out of the autumn mist she forgot all about the funny feeling of being so high in the air, and gave a little squeak of excitement. 'Ooh, we're going on *holiday*,' she said happily.

Suddenly they were in the middle of swirling clouds. 'It's all right, we're going down,' explained Great Uncle Bulgaria. But he looked a little pale. Then there was the airstrip in front of them, looking much too tiny for the plane, even if it *was* very small, but down it came with hardly a bump.

'*Alors, mille mercis,*' murmured Madame Cholet as they came to a halt. Miss Adelaide, ably assisted by Tobermory, had certainly planned everything extremely well, for there was a small, if rather battered, car to meet the Wimbledon Wombles. Hunched over the steering wheel was a very small grey-brown Womble who said shyly:

'I'm Second Cousin Corbletts Womble. Very glad and pleased to have you here, eh?'

'And we are particularly glad and proud to *be* here,' said Great Uncle Bulgaria, who was all ready to make a speech. 'Furthermore . . .'

'Not now, Bulgaria,' said Madame Cholet, 'I, for one, am exhausted . . .'

'Of course, of course,' said Great Uncle Bulgaria, 'I was quite forgetting, Madame Cholet, that *you* are not used to flying. Drive on, Second Cousin Corbletts.'

Tomsk and Alderney didn't say a word; they just sat and shivered and bumped up and down while their round little eyes looked from side to side at this new world.

And there was a great deal to look *at*. Cobbled streets and little houses painted in all kinds of pretty colours. Big hills covered in bracken, castles and forts jutting right out into the purple, blue sea, frothing waves and stretches of yellow sand, dotted about with fierce grey rocks.

45

'It's not a *bit* like Wimbledon Common,' said Alderney.

So what with looking at things and wondering what their cousins had got ready for them, it hardly seemed any time at all before they finally arrived at the main island burrow. It smelt a little salty, but apart from that it was delightfully familiar with its neat, well-kept rooms, and a Workshop which was just as organized as Tobermory's but full of nets and seaweed pots which needed repairing. While as for the kitchen . . .

'*Mais c'est merveilleux!*' exclaimed Madame Cholet, clasping her front paws together.

'*Pardon Madame*,' said a very small shy voice, 'but I am Madame Blaye. My cooking is *comme-ci comme-ça*, and not at all as good as yours. How often have I admired your recipe for Moss Pie which is famous throughout all the Womble world...'

'It is nothing,' said Madame Cholet ...

'But yes it is. Should you give me the honour I would wish to show you my seaweed blancmange which I am now making. If you would care to come this way ...'

And Madame Blaye, who was quite tiny, stood shyly to one side and bowed Madame Cholet into her kitchen.

Great Uncle Bulgaria was also enjoying his visit as he sat and rocked backwards and forwards in the study of Great Uncle Clonque. Great Uncle Clonque always wore a white panama hat, whatever the weather. Great Uncle Bulgaria didn't always follow every word that his new friend said, as this venerable Womble sometimes spoke in the old Alderney *patois* – an offshoot of Norman French, but overall they understood each other pretty well as they gossiped about how times had changed, how Human Beings were becoming more wasteful and untidy every year, and how much better everything had been when they were young, well over two hundred years ago.

'Things aren't the same, eh?' said Great Uncle Clonque.

'Not what they were,' agreed Great Uncle Bulgaria, and then added politely, 'eh?'

It was all very restful.

But for Alderney and Tomsk it was also most exciting.

There were ancient Womble burrows to be explored, rocks to be climbed and paddling, swimming and surfing to be enjoyed. Alderney wasn't much good at surfing – Tomsk soon excelled at this – but Alderney, much to her own surprise, soon discovered that she was extremely good at collecting, sorting and cooking all kinds of seaweed.

So, what with one thing and another, the whole fortnight seemed to whizz past until it came to the last evening. Great Uncle Bulgaria could no longer be restrained. He made a long speech of thanks to the Alderney Island Wombles, interrupted from time to time by cries of 'Hear, hear', and 'Ho, ho, ho', by Longis Womble (who was always rather noisy and had to be 'shushed' by Madame Blaye) and then there was a return speech by Great Uncle Clonque, and that was followed by an exchange of gifts. What with one thing and another there was a great deal of sniffing and blowing into handkerchiefs until everybody laughed as Tomsk and Alderney sang a song they had composed themselves and which began:

'There are Wombles everywhere, particularly here . . .'

And so, exactly two weeks after their departure, the four Wimbledon Wombles returned from their island holiday looking fit, younger and amazingly healthy.

'Wombles of Wimbledon,' said Great Uncle Bulgaria, 'we've had a very good holiday with our fellow Channel Island Wombles who have been very, very kind to us. However, it's even nicer to be home. What is more we have a great deal to tell you about new ideas, new recipes and lots of material for a little constructional plan of mine . . . but as you all look a bit weary . . . we'll leave all that until tomorrow . . .'

48

Seaside Assortment

The Wombles had collected a great deal of interesting bits and pieces on holiday, and Great Uncle Bulgaria organized them into a Seaside Scrapbook. (You should try this – it is a good way of remembering some of the best things about a holiday.) With a great deal of pencil-licking, Tomsk had written out a little chart to show how his swimming had improved. Alderney had made a shell collection with the name of each shell written neatly underneath. But with the help of Tobermory, they had both had an idea for using their finds in a way that *all* the burrow could share . . .

A Womble Collage

A collage is a collection of bits and pieces arranged together in patterns on a piece of stiff card to make a picture. You can use anything you like as long as it will stick on the card and has an interesting shape, colour, or texture. The young Wombles decided to make their collage mainly from natural objects but you can choose your own materials.

YOU WILL NEED

1. A strong piece of stiffened card. For a small collage, the side of a cereal packet is ideal

2. Strong scissors

3. White powder-paint or similar
   Or wallpaper lining paper. This you may be lucky enough to find at home, otherwise you can get it at a do-it-yourself shop

49

Or sugar paper from an art shop
Or part of an old sheet, or a piece of hessian or clean sacking. You must cut the material or the paper so that it is 5 cm longer and wider than your card

4. PVA glue or similar and small spreaders for using it

5. Leaves, flowers (don't choose large flower heads such as chrysanthemums, or ones with sappy stems like dandelions which do not press very well), nutshells split in half, seeds (e.g. split peas, lentils, dried beans, mustard seeds, sunflower seeds, seedpods), crushed eggshells, feathers, twigs, cork, bark, and if, like the Wombles you have recently been to the seaside, you could also use sand, dried seaweed, shells, little bits of driftwood, smooth glass and small pebbles

6. Paper: tissue paper, metal foil, crêpe or corrugated paper. Use lots of different colours

7. Cling-wrap plastic film (used to keep food fresh). This you can buy from the local hardware shop or even a large supermarket

WHAT YOU DO

1. First press your leaves and flowers. Take a sheet of white paper and on it arrange the leaves or flowers you want to press. Now put a sheet of blotting paper on top of them and press them either inside or underneath a heavy book. (Great Uncle Bulgaria allowed Tomsk to use his *Great Atlas of the World* because, if you are careful, it doesn't hurt the book.)

Leave them for about ten days. They are now ready to be used in your collage.

2. Either paint your card white, or cover it with the paper or material you have cut to size. Spread the paper over the card, fold it round the edges and glue firmly. Do exactly the same with the material, if this is the background you prefer. Pressed leaves or flowers look well on white paper, but the heavier or more colourful objects will look good on the material. Natural objects often look better on a light-coloured background because their colours tend to be soft, but you can add splashes of brighter colour with the different sorts of paper and metal foil.

3. Now using your spreader, glue whatever objects you have chosen on to your background. To glue the sand and lighter materials, remember to put glue on your background and then lightly press things on to it. It often pays to think a bit before you start and work out some kind of overall pattern.

4. Leave your collage to dry for several hours.

5. Finally, you can keep all the loose ends secure and give your collage a professional, glossy finish by covering it with the cling-wrap plastic film.

A Merry Wombling Christmas

ALL THE YOUNG WOMBLES in the burrow could sense that Christmas was coming, because they had delightful tingling feelings up and down their backs, and there was a very exciting atmosphere in the burrow. Even the older Wombles were aware of it and as Great Uncle Bulgaria said to Tobermory:

'I may be getting on a bit . . .'

'That's right,' agreed Tobermory, 'why, you must be about two hundred and . . . and . . .' and then he stopped counting Great Uncle Bulgaria's age on his paws, because it's not very polite to work out older Wombles' ages *exactly*.

'Getting on a bit,' proceeded Great Uncle Bulgaria when he was quite sure that Tobermory had stopped counting, 'but I still enjoy Christmas enormously. This year I thought we might plan something extra special.'

'Such as what?' asked Tobermory.

'That,' said Great Uncle Bulgaria, 'I will leave you to think about, Tobermory. Naturally, if I have any particularly good ideas or notions I shall pass them on to you.'

'Ta very much,' said Tobermory as Great Uncle Bulgaria

left the Workshop. 'Well, I dunno, what extra special something can *I* possibly think up? It's not as if I haven't got enough to do, what with all this rubbish piled up and waiting to be sorted, let alone all the repairing and repapering that needs to be done in the burrow. I dunno,' and Tobermory scratched his head, tilting back his bowler hat and making his grey fur stand up on end. 'Problems, problems,' he muttered and went to see Madame Cholet.

The Womble kitchen smelt even spicier and more delicious than usual.

'Cor,' said Tobermory, 'Madame Cholet, I can see *you* are going to make this an extra-special Christmas all right, and that's really why I'm here. Great Uncle Bulgaria wants me to make this an extra-special Christmas all round, but frankly I don't know how to go about it and that's a fact!'

'*Tiens!*' said Madame Cholet. 'I don't see how I can help you, M'sieur Tobermory. I wish I could. But all I can do to make it special-extra is to cook even more, and – believe me, for it is the absolute truth – I have enough to do already! *La petite* Alderney is assisting me, of course, but even so . . .' And Madame Cholet's shoulders went right up to her ears.

'P'raps Miss Adelaide'll have some ideas,' said Tobermory. 'Ta very much, Madame Cholet.'

Miss Adelaide was in the Womblegarten absolutely surrounded by paper-chains and bits and pieces of Christmas decorations. She never stopped work, sorting and cutting and sticking, while Tobermory sat down and told her about this extra-special Christmas notion.

'Well I really cannot give you any practical advice,' said

Miss Adelaide at the finish, and then, nodding at Tomsk who was slowly and carefully cutting up bits of newspaper, she added, 'as I have more than enough to do here. Steady Tomsk. Don't cut up too much. Christmas is a particularly busy period for me, you know, as apart from correcting all last term's work I have to plan next term's classes. Indeed,' and Miss Adelaide's ramrod-straight back actually sagged a tiny bit, 'I have more than enough to do, what with one thing and another!'

Tobermory returned slowly to his Workshop, and in spite of the excitement of Christmas he was quite snappy with Wellington who was sitting at a bench trying to get some Christmas-tree lights repaired.

'Sorry,' said Wellington, who actually had nothing to be sorry about as he hadn't done anything wrong. 'Is something the matter, Tobermory?'

'Only problems, problems,' sighed Tobermory. 'How can we make this an extra-special Christmas when there is so much ordinary work still to be done? What's more, young Womble, you'll never get those lights properly fixed if you unwind the bulb that way, tck, tck, tck . . .'

'Sorry,' said Wellington.

'I'd better go and have a word with Great Uncle Bulgaria,' said Tobermory. 'Not that I want to, but I'd better . . .'

By this time even Great Uncle Bulgaria was not quite his usual unruffled self, for when Tobermory entered his office he discovered his old friend rocking backwards and forwards very fast, which was always a bad sign. Tobermory stood in the doorway for a moment or two, and then he realized what was wrong.

Bungo and Orinoco were trying to sort out all the pages of Great Uncle Bulgaria's Christmas speech and were getting them into a fine old mess. Added to which they had upset the big bran tub out of which all the Wombles always took a lucky dip to get their own particular Christmas present. So there were pieces of paper, pawfuls of bran and half-done-up gifts all over the floor.

'Oh dear,' said Tobermory. He tried to escape out of the door again, but Great Uncle Bulgaria had spotted him.

'Tobermory,' said Great Uncle Bulgaria awfully, 'I want a few words with you! Orinoco!'

Orinoco jumped violently.

'Bungo!'

'Yes!' exclaimed Bungo, jumping so much that even more pages of the Christmas speech went flying.

'Out, out, out!' ordered Great Uncle Bulgaria, pointing at the door with his stick. Bungo and Orinoco fled.

They didn't stop fleeing until they reached the Playroom, where they found Tomsk doing exercises on the wall bars and Wellington playing Wombles cat's-cradle (which is Wellington's own invention and very clever and interesting) with Alderney. All the young Wombles began talking at once and complaining and explaining about what an awful sort of day it had been in spite of Christmas being very close.

'I'll tell you what's wrong,' said Alderney. 'It's Madame Cholet having too much cooking to do. I think I could do all that cooking myself really, because I'm not bad at it and . . .'

'It's not that at all,' said Tomsk in his slow, rumbling voice. 'It's Miss Adelaide who can't get through everything. She's got such a lot to arrange, so how can she make all the decorations and that and . . .'

'Sorry,' interrupted Wellington, 'but honestly, that's not the trouble. The trouble is that Tobermory has got too much

clearing up and sorting to do and I think . . .'

'Get on,' put in Orinoco and Bungo with one voice. 'It's Great Uncle Bulgaria who has got too much work to do and . . .'

For at least ten minutes all the young Wombles continued to talk at once. When at last they paused for breath there were a few seconds of silence and then suddenly a high squeaky voice said:

'I'll tell you all what, why don't *we* plan this extra-special Christmas. Come on, let's!'

Practically everybody looked at Bungo. But Bungo only shook his head and pointed at Wellington, who was standing up very straight with his eyes shining.

'We could do it,' said Wellington, who was shivering with excitement. 'Between us we could do everything extra-special and give all the older Wombles a lovely rest. It'd be marvellous fun. Oh, do let's try. Alderney can do the cooking and Tomsk the decorations and me the Womble lights and Orinoco the bran tub and Bungo . . .'

'What?' said Bungo, who was a bit put out that he hadn't thought of all this himself.

'You can make the speech,' said Wellington.

'All right, I agree,' said Bungo, before anybody else had drawn breath.

It was a most exciting idea and there was a great deal of talk and discussion and quite a bit of arguing, but the result was that the following morning Great Uncle Bulgaria, Madame Cholet, Miss Adelaide and Tobermory found a notice pinned to the Workshop door which said:

THIS IS GOING TO BE AN EXTRA-SPECIAL CHRISTMAS. ORGANIZED BY ALL THE UNDER SINGED . . . (Miss Adelaide re-spelt that) PLEASE ALL OTHER WOMBLES DON'T DO ANYTHING!!!

'Dear me,' said Great Uncle Bulgaria, reading through this twice. 'Dear, dear me . . . well perhaps we should let them get on with it, eh, Madame Cholet, Miss Adelaide, Tobermory?'

The three elderly Wombles looked at each other, thought deeply, then looked at each other again, and smiled.

So Great Uncle Bulgaria solemnly got out his fountain pen and wrote at the bottom of the notice:

AGREED. BULGARIA COBURG WOMBLE.

The young Wombles were beside themselves with excitement and importance but, as Wellington soon discovered, it was one thing to have a good idea and quite another to make it work smoothly. Tobermory kindly let him take over one of the smaller workrooms as an office and Wellington furnished it with a desk that had been made out of bits of packing cases, a stool and an enormous cardboard notice board. This board quickly became covered with all kinds of lists and instructions about who was supposed to be doing what.

It all looked most efficient on paper and it started off very well; but before long snags started developing. Tomsk went on quietly making decorations; but he ran out of paste and, when he went to see Alderney for some more, she snapped at him because she'd made such an enormous blueberry, bramble and gorse Christmas cake that it didn't look as if she would ever get it in the oven, and she was very worried about it. Tomsk had to make his own paste and he put in too much grassflour, so the paste set as hard as concrete and that made the decorations very thick and heavy. Quite a bit of paste set hard on Tomsk too, as he had covered himself in it. So, grumbling and muttering, he went off to the Common to look for pieces of wood with which to make a special sort of Christmas tree. He also hoped to wash away some of the paste, since it was raining heavily. He quite forgot that, according to the list, he was supposed to be helping Orinoco with the bran tub.

'That's right, leave me to do everything,' grumbled Orinoco, when a thorough search of the burrow failed to disclose the missing Tomsk, 'and there's all the presents to be done up yet. Never mind, p'raps Bungo'll lend me a paw.'

'Can't,' snapped Bungo, in just the same sort of voice that Alderney had used earlier to Tomsk. 'I've only made three crackers so far; I'd no idea they were so difficult to do. They didn't *look* difficult when Tobermory was making 'em last year. I can't understand it.' And Bungo heaved such an enormous sigh that it raised him right up on to his back paws.

'Why not give it a rest and help me with the bran tub?' suggested Orinoco artfully.

'Oh, drat the presents. *You* do 'em. That's *your* job! I haven't written a word of my speech yet either.'

'Drat your silly old speech,' retorted Orinoco. 'You always talk enough. Yackity-yackity-yackity . . .'

Regretfully, at this point Bungo picked up a rather lumpy looking cracker and hit Orinoco over the head with it, so Orinoco pulled it away from him and hit Bungo, and in two seconds flat they were swiping left and right until a very loud . . .

'Ho hum, tck, tck, tck . . .' out in the passage made them both stop instantly. The crackers had come completely to bits, there were pieces of paper everywhere, and the room was a mess. Bungo opened his mouth to say:

60

'You can jolly well help me clear this up . . .'

But Orinoco, with a surprising burst of speed, had vanished. He had gone tearing past Great Uncle Bulgaria so fast that the old Womble had to hold on to his hat to stop it blowing off.

'Wellington!' panted Orinoco, bursting into the Christmas office. 'You've got to tell Bungo – Owwwww!'

Wellington had at that precise moment just finished mending the Christmas lights and was about to test the last one before switching them on. Orinoco's whirlwind entrance, however, made him jump violently, his elbow hit the switch, there was a tremendous 'zzzz', a very bright light for half a second and then . . . total darkness as every light in the burrow fused.

What Wellington then said to Orinoco and what Orinoco replied is best forgotten. How Tomsk, who was just returning with a load of wood, dripping wet and still coated in concrete paste, collided with Bungo in the sudden darkness and sent the bran tub flying is also better forgotten. As for poor Alderney, she threw her apron over her head for she was sure she could hear her lovely cake slowly collapsing in the cooling oven.

'Tck, tck, tck,' said Great Uncle Bulgaria, reaching for the Wimbledon Borough Council lantern, which he always kept for emergencies, and lighting it. 'Tck, tck, tck. It is going to be a very special Christmas and no mistake. Never mind, the experience will do them all good!'

Naturally all the young Wombles blamed each other, but somehow they managed to sort themselves out and to start all over again, and to their great credit not one of them went and complained to an older Womble.

'We'll just have to work as a team,' said Wellington, crossing out his lists and re-writing them. 'We'll ALL go and help Alderney with the cooking, then we'll all go and help Tomsk with the decorations and . . .'

'We'll all do up presents,' put in Orinoco quickly.

'And p'raps we'd all better write the speech,' said Bungo, who had so far written one word. It was 'A'.

The teamwork was a bit ragged to begin with, but it got better and better, even if there was a fair amount of squabbling.

Then, quite suddenly it seemed, it *was* Christmas.

And what a Christmas! For a start there were decorations (somewhat lumpy and heavy in parts) absolutely everywhere. There was a simply enormous and most unusual home-made Christmas tree covered with sparkling lights and a bran tub quite stuffed with exactly the presents that every Womble had ever really wanted. There were two crackers for every Womble, complete with a tiny gift, a paper hat, a banger and a motto. (One of Orinoco's read: 'What is better than forty winks? Eighty winks!') And to top it all, Alderney's cake was found to be cooked right through, quite delicious and so big that as Madame Cholet whispered to Miss Adelaide:

'It will last us until Easter at least. *Tiens!*'

'*Alors,*' agreed Miss Adelaide in a very correct accent. 'Now Bungo is going to make his speech. One wonders what he will say.'

'Ahem,' said Bungo, looking round. He sounded unusually nervous for him and everybody stopped chattering and went very quiet.

'This speech,' said Bungo, in a high voice which he hardly recognized as his own, 'was written by all of us – Alderney, Wellington, Tomsk, Orinoco, and me. It's this. "A very happy happy Christmas, Wombles".' Bungo sat down with a thump.

There was a moment's silence and then tremendous applause with all the Wombles clapping and shouting and stamping their paws. The noise only died down when Great Uncle Bulgaria rose slowly to his back paws.

The old Womble looked at the decorations, the sparkling tree, the presents, the crackers, the remains of the food and at the dozens of little furry faces and the dozens of pairs of shining eyes as round as buttons.

'Here we go,' said Tobermory out of the corner of his mouth to Miss Adelaide who replied 'shhhh' so severely that Tobermory subsided instantly.

'This is *my* Christmas speech,' said Great Uncle Bulgaria. 'I am very, very proud of my young working Wombles. I always said this would be an extra-special Christmas – and so it is. Thank you, and I'm sure you'll all agree with me.'

And everybody did. It *had* been an extra-special sort of Christmas. But then Great Uncle Bulgaria had a quite uncanny gift of always being right . . .

64